Dear Parent:

Congratulations! Your child is taking the first steps on an exciting journey. The destination? Independent reading!

STEP INTO READING® will help your child get there. The program offers five steps to reading success. Each step includes fun stories and colorful art. There are also Step into Reading Sticker Books, Step into Reading Math Readers, Step into Reading Phonics Readers, Step into Reading Write-In Readers, and Step into Reading Phonics Boxed Sets—a complete literacy program with something for every child.

Learning to Read, Step by Step!

Ready to Read   Preschool–Kindergarten
• big type and easy words • rhyme and rhythm • picture clues
For children who know the alphabet and are eager to begin reading.

Reading with Help   Preschool–Grade 1
• basic vocabulary • short sentences • simple stories
For children who recognize familiar words and sound out new words with help.

Reading on Your Own   Grades 1–3
• engaging characters • easy-to-follow plots • popular topics
For children who are ready to read on their own.

Reading Paragraphs   Grades 2–3
• challenging vocabulary • short paragraphs • exciting stories
For newly independent readers who read simple sentences with confidence.

Ready for Chapters   Grades 2–4
• chapters • longer paragraphs • full-color art
For children who want to take the plunge into chapter books but still like colorful pictures.

STEP INTO READING® is designed to give every child a successful reading experience. The grade levels are only guides. Children can progress through the steps at their own speed, developing confidence in their reading, no matter what their grade.

Remember, a lifetime love of reading starts with a single step!

Published in the United States by Random House Children's Books, a division of Random House, Inc., 1745 Broadway, New York, NY 10019, and in Canada by Random House of Canada Limited, Toronto. Step into Reading, Random House, and the Random House colophon are registered trademarks of Random House, Inc. Nickelodeon, Teenage Mutant Ninja Turtles, and all related titles, logos, and characters are trademarks of Viacom International Inc. and Viacom Overseas Holdings C.V.

Visit us on the Web!
StepIntoReading.com
randomhouse.com/kids

Educators and librarians, for a variety of teaching tools, visit us at RHTeachersLibrarians.com

ISBN: 978-0-307-98070-0

Printed in the United States of America 10 9 8 7 6 5 4 3 2 1

nickelodeon
TEENAGE MUTANT NINJA TURTLES

GREEN TEAM!

Adapted by Christy Webster

Illustrated by Patrick Spaziante

Based on the screenplays by Joshua Sternin and J. R. Ventimilia
Based on characters by Peter Laird and Kevin Eastman

Random House 🏠 New York

A long time ago, a man named Hamato Yoshi bought four turtles at a pet store. As he left, he passed a man on the street who was walking in a strange way, almost like a robot. Hamato decided to follow him.

In an alley, a rat ran up Hamato's leg. The strange man saw Hamato and threw a canister at him. *Smash!* It broke, splashing green goo all over Hamato, the turtles, and the rat. The goo caused a chemical reaction. The turtles grew to human size, and Hamato grew fur and a tail. He became a human rat!

That day, Hamato and the turtles became mutants.

Now Hamato Yoshi is called Splinter. For fifteen years, he and the Turtles all lived together in the sewer.

The Turtles called Splinter "Sensei," which means "teacher." He was teaching the Turtles how to be ninjas!

They were the Teenage Mutant Ninja Turtles.

Leonardo was brave.
Michelangelo liked to have fun.

Donatello was smart and loved gadgets.
Raphael was tough.

On their fifteenth birthday, the Turtles wanted to see the City. The Turtles had never been aboveground. Splinter thought people would be afraid of them.

"Do you think we're ready, Sensei?" Leonardo asked.

"Yes and no," Splinter replied. In the end, he let them go. "Don't let anyone see you," he warned.

The Turtles cheered.

The Turtles peeked out a manhole and saw the street for the first time. It was dark and spooky. There was dirt and garbage everywhere.

"It's so beautiful," Michelangelo said.

The Turtles ran around the city, exploring. They peered in a store window. "Look at the computers!" Donatello said.

Suddenly, the Turtles saw a bright light. It was a a scooter. The man riding it couldn't believe his eyes. Raphael growled at him. The man screamed and swerved. He just missed hitting the Turtles!

A box fell off the scooter as the man drove away.

The Turtles moved on. But Michelangelo grabbed the box.

The Turtles looked at the box.

"Should we open it?" Donatello asked.

Raphael opened the box. Inside was a pizza! The Turtles had never seen pizza before.

"I think it's food," Donatello said.

Michelangelo took a bite. It was awesome!

"I love it up here!" Michelangelo said.

The Turtles gobbled the whole pizza.

When the sun started to rise, it was time to go home. On their way there, Donatello saw a girl walking with her dad. The girl's name was April.

"She's the most beautiful girl I've ever seen," he said.

"She's the *only* girl you've ever seen," Raphael said.

Suddenly, strangers drove up and tried to capture April and her dad. April screamed for help.

"We have to save them!" Donatello cried.

"Splinter says we can't be seen," Leonardo said.

Donatello rushed toward the van anyway. The other Turtles ran after him.

The Turtles tried to save April and
her dad from the bad guys. But they kept
bumping into each other.

Leonardo jabbed Raphael. "Watch it!"
he said.

Michelangelo knocked Donatello over.
"Whoops!" Michelangelo said.

The Turtles couldn't work as a team. The bad guys got away with April and her dad.

One bad guy stayed behind. Michelangelo chased him into an alley and finally won the fight. Then a weird pink blob crawled out of the man's chest.

The bad guy was a robot with a brain inside!

The brain hissed and jumped up. Michelangelo screamed.

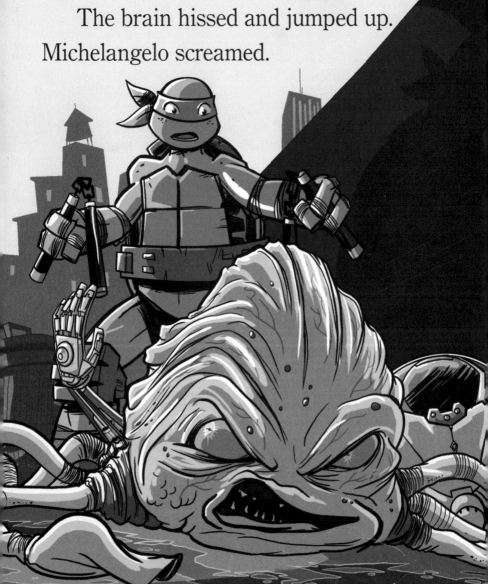

Michelangelo rushed over to the other Turtles. He tried to tell them what he had seen.

"That thing had a brain," he said, but the other Turtles didn't believe him.

"We all have brains," Leonardo replied.

Back in the sewer, the Turtles told Splinter about April and her dad. They told him how they couldn't work together.

"I need to train you as a team," Splinter said. "Next year you can go to the surface again."

Donatello didn't want to wait a year. He wanted to save April.

There was no time for Splinter to train them. But Splinter thought they would be a better team if they had a leader. He chose Leonardo.

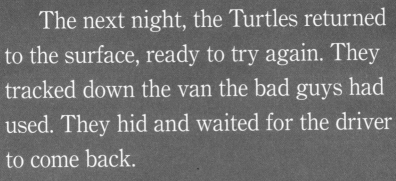

The next night, the Turtles returned to the surface, ready to try again. They tracked down the van the bad guys had used. They hid and waited for the driver to come back.

When he saw the driver coming, Leonardo said, "I have a daring plan." But the other Turtles were already running toward the van!

The driver saw the Turtles coming for him. He jumped into the van and sped away.

The Turtles chased after the van. They jumped over rooftops to keep up. Leonardo threw a star. The tire blew! The van swerved and crashed.

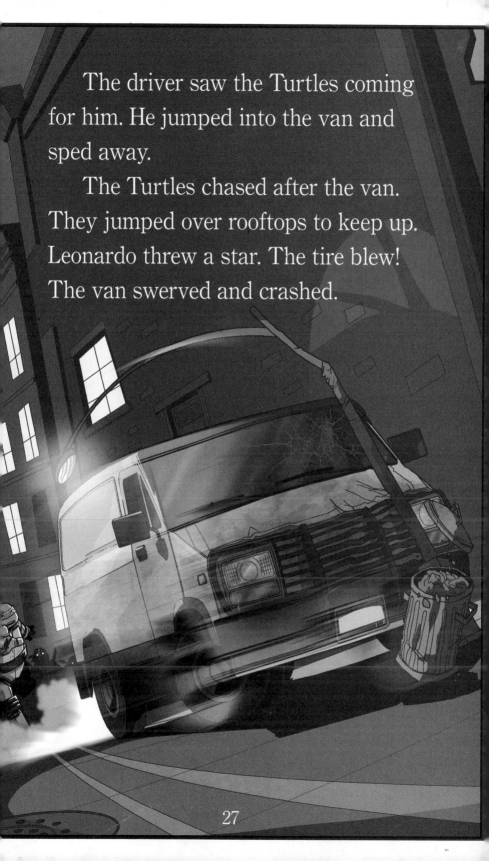

Raphael opened the back of the van. It was full of the same green goo that had turned the Turtles into mutants!

"This is huge," Leonardo said. "These bad guys have something to do with us."

"How is that possible?" Donatello asked.

"Anything is possible for alien robots!" Michelangelo said. He grabbed the driver and starting pulling on his face. He wanted to show the other Turtles how the bad guys had pink brains inside!

But the driver's face was real. It didn't come off.

"Okay, but those other men were totally robots," Michelangelo said.

Raphael took a canister of green goo from the van. He shoved it in the driver's face. "This stuff can turn you into a mutant like us," he said. "Tell us what's going on." He tipped the canister a little.

"Okay!" the driver said. "My name is Snake. Those guys are called the Kraang. They're grabbing scientists. I don't know why."

He showed the Turtles the Kraang's hideout. Raphael wanted to attack right away. But Leonardo wanted to make a plan first. While they were arguing, Snake escaped!

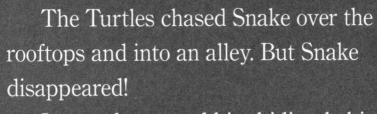

The Turtles chased Snake over the rooftops and into an alley. But Snake disappeared!

Leonardo spotted him hiding behind some trash cans. He nudged Raphael. "Oh, great," Leonardo said loudly. "We let him get away."

"Let's drive the van up to the gate at midnight," Leonardo said. Snake heard him.

Later, at the Kraang's hideout, the van was racing up to the door. Snake and the Kraang thought it was the Turtles.

Zap! The Kraang destroyed the van. It crashed into the gate. Green goo splashed everywhere and covered Snake.

But the van was empty. Where were the Turtles?

"That was lucky," said Michelangelo.

"That was the plan!" said Leonardo.

They sneaked into the hideout. It was full of the Kraang! They were running all over the place. One by one, the Turtles took out the Kraang.

The final Kraang sparked and came apart. Its brain crawled out!

"See?" Michelangelo said. He picked up the brain. "I told you!"

The other Turtles screamed. The Kraang really were robot aliens with brains!

The Turtles searched the hideout for April and her dad. They found a holding cell. April and her dad were inside! Donatello tried to pick the lock. It wouldn't open.

Raphael started smashing it! Just as the door was about to give, the Kraang came back. They dragged April and her dad away.

The Turtles chased them outside.
Snake blocked their path. But now he was
huge. He was covered in leaves and thorns.
The green goo had mutated him!

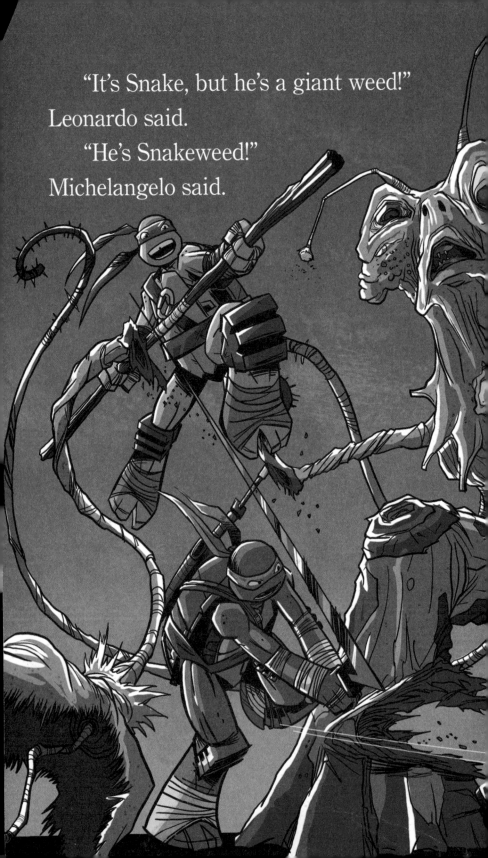

"It's Snake, but he's a giant weed!"
Leonardo said.

"He's Snakeweed!"
Michelangelo said.

The Turtles tried to fight past Snakeweed. Every time they sliced a branch, it grew back.

"No fair!" Donatello said.

The Kraang forced April and her dad into a helicopter. Donatello leaped into the air and grabbed the helicopter's skids. The other Turtles stayed behind, holding back Snakeweed and the Kraang.

The helicopter swerved with Donatello's weight. April fell out! Donatello jumped after her. He saved her!

The Kraang were everywhere. The
Turtles were trapped between them and
Snakeweed. Snakeweed yanked Leonardo
by the ankle and swung him upside down.
Leonardo spotted some power lines. They
led to a big power generator.

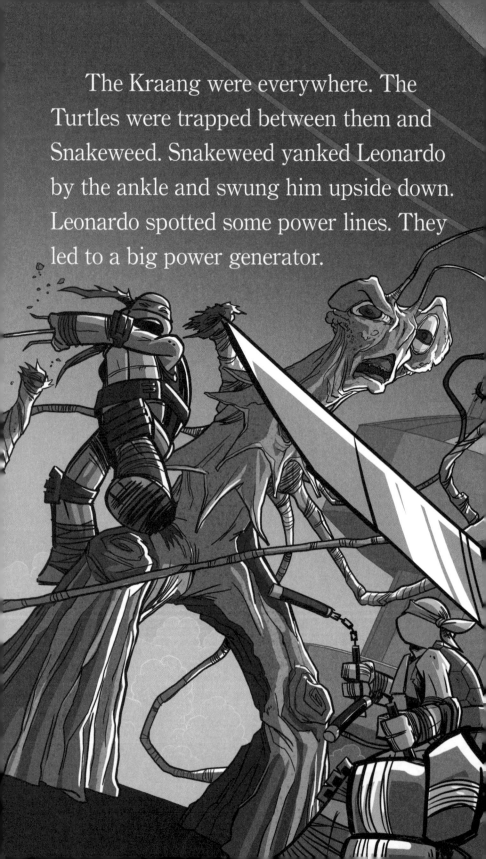

"I have a plan!" he yelled. He told
Raphael and Michelangelo what it was
as he broke free from Snakeweed.

Raphael and Michelangelo stayed near Snakeweed. Leonardo climbed the generator. Donatello and April watched.

"What are they doing?" Donatello asked.

Snakeweed chased Leonardo to the generator. So did the Kraang. They almost had him. *Blam!* Just as their energy cannon blasted, Leonardo jumped out of the way.

The generator exploded! The Turtles and April ran away.

April was safe, thanks to the Teenage Mutant Ninja Turtles.

But the Kraang still had her dad.

"We'll help him," Donatello told her.

"But it's not your fight," April said.

"It is now," they said.

Now the Turtles are a team!